What I Want To Be

By P. Mignon Hinds
Illustrated by Cornelius Van Wright

This Golden Book® was published in cooperation with Essence Communications, Inc.

 A Golden Book • New York

Western Publishing Company, Inc., Racine, Wisconsin 53404

Library of Congress Catalog Card Number: 94-79636   ISBN: 0-307-11439-2   A MCMXCV

I love to visit Grandma on Saturdays. We cuddle on her big blue couch and talk for hours and hours.

One Saturday I wore my new space ring. Grandma noticed it right away. "Maya, when your daddy was a little boy, he had a space ring, too," she told me. "He wanted to be an astronaut when he grew up. He also wanted to be a police officer and a baseball player."

Grandma and I laughed. Then she asked me, "What do you want to be?"

"I don't know," I said. I like to do so many things.

Grandma thought Daddy's ring might still be in the attic. So I ran upstairs to see.

I found a big black trunk. It was full of great stuff—lots of old clothes and toys. I was hoping Daddy's ring would be in there, too.

Right on top was an explorer's hat and a shovel. I
pulled them out of the trunk and began to imagine
what it would be like to be an explorer. . . .
I could search for treasures in faraway places.
I'd dig up things people made long ago.

Then I dug deeper into the trunk and came up
with some swimming goggles and flippers. I put
on the flippers and could almost feel myself
gliding through the water. . . .

If I were an underwater scientist, I could
swim in the ocean and get to know all kinds
of fish, and maybe even a whale!

Next I found this cool red fire truck and a firefighter's helmet. . . .

If I were a firefighter, I would have to be very brave. I'd jump into my fire truck whenever the alarm rang and rush to the rescue.

Inside the trunk were some fancy things, too—
Grandma's old dresses and a pretty lace shawl. . . .
Maybe I could be a dress designer and make beautiful
clothes. Everybody would want to wear something
made by Maya!

But maybe it's more exciting to be an animal doctor at a zoo. . . .

Imagine me helping lions and tigers stay healthy and happy. "Take a deep breath," I'd say to the elephant.

I could be a baseball player, too. . . .
Every time I hit a home run, I'd wave to Daddy
in the stands.

I never did find Daddy's ring. But I did find this toy rocket!

If I were an astronaut, I would travel to the moon and stars. Three, two, one, blast off!

At last, at the bottom of the trunk were some of Daddy's old books. As I put the rocket and other things back, I had one more thought. . . .

Maybe I could be a writer. I could write funny stories, animal stories, all kinds of stories.

I was thinking about my stories when I heard Grandma calling. I ran downstairs. I could hardly wait to tell her all the things I want to be!

Grandma gave me a hug when I told her my dreams. "You can be whatever you want to be, Maya," she said. "And whatever you choose, always do your best."

I nodded my head and hugged her back.

Then she added, "But there's one thing you'll always be— Grandma's special girl."